Princess Truly

I Can Build It!

BY
Kelly
Greenawalt

ART BY
Amariah
Rauscher

🌽 ACORN™
SCHOLASTIC INC.

To Heather O'Wrigley, the best friend a girl
could ever have. — KG

For Jude, the best builder. — AR

Text copyright © 2020 by Kelly Greenawalt
Illustrations copyright © 2020 by Amariah Rauscher

Library of Congress Cataloging-in-Publication Data

Names: Greenawalt, Kelly, author. | Rauscher, Amariah, illustrator.
Title: I can build it! / by Kelly Greenawalt ; illustrated by Amariah Rauscher.
Description: First edition. | New York, NY : Acorn/Scholastic Inc., 2020. |
Series: Princess Truly ; 3 | Summary: In rhyming text Princess Truly, super girl, uses her magic curls
to build things, including a bike for her brother, who has outgrown his old one,
and a super snack machine.
Identifiers: LCCN 2019007624 | ISBN 9781338340099 (pbk. : alk. paper) | ISBN 9781338340112
(hardcover : alk. paper)
Subjects: LCSH: Princesses—Juvenile fiction. | African Americans—Juvenile fiction. | Superheroes—
Juvenile fiction. | Inventions—Juvenile fiction. | Stories in rhyme. | CYAC: Stories in rhyme. |
Princesses—Fiction. | African Americans—Fiction. | Superheroes—Fiction. | Inventions—Fiction. |
LCGFT: Stories in rhyme.
Classification: LCC PZ8.3.G7495 Iaj 2020 | DDC [E]--dc23
LC record available at https://lccn.loc.gov/2019007624

10 9 8 7 6 5 4 3 2 1   20 21 22 23 24

Printed in China   62

First edition, March 2020

Edited by Rachel Matson
Book design by Sarah Dvojack

Truly Great Ideas

I am Princess Truly.
I have a helpful heart.

I build exciting things.

I'm curious and smart.

First, I have an idea.

Then I draw up the plans.

Next, I find all my tools

and build things with my hands.

Come and see my workshop.
My curls begin to glow.

We will take the Zip-Hop.

Up to the top we go!

See all that I have made.
Come on, let's look around!

I built lots of new things
with old things I have found.

9

Come take a look at this,
the Brushy-Brush Machine.

It is very handy.
It makes our teeth so clean.

I built that robot, too,
and this purple race car.

I build amazing things.
I am a shining star!

Super Cool Racers

This is my brother, Ty.
His old bike is too small.

He wants to ride with me,
but he thinks he might fall.

15

I have a great idea.
My magical curls shine.

I will build a racer.
A super cool design.

I add two extra wheels
because Ty is learning.

Now he will not fall down,
even when he is turning.

I add turbo power.
This bike is built to race.

Ty can ride super fast
and zoom from place to place.

I add an umbrella.
It will help Ty stay dry.

I add a propeller.

It will make his bike fly!

Ty wants to have a race.
I know just what to do!

I build a bike for me.
So I can go fast, too!

We speed up the big hill.
We launch into the sky.

With my rainbow power,
our super bikes can fly.

The Super Snack Machine

These cute pets need our help.
We go there right away.

There is a lot to do.
This might take us all day!

We give the cats a bath,

then walk the pups out back.

Next, we mop up the mess.

Now it's time for a snack.

Yikes! The box is empty.
The jar is empty, too.

There are no bones or treats.
What are we going to do?

I have a great idea.
My magic curls shine bright.

We all work super fast,
until it is just right.

35

start

SUPER SNACK MACHINE

The Super Snack Machine!
It can scoop, mix, and make.

It has rainbow power.
It takes no time to bake.

start

SUPER SNACK MACHINE

I press the start button.
The snack machine twinkles.

It swirls on the icing,
then shakes on the sprinkles.

A snack for every pet!
Pink bones for the poodles.

They wag their happy tails
and dance with Sir Noodles.

I am Princess Truly.

I am caring and smart.

Princess
Truly's
Puppy-
Rocking
Bed

I can build anything,
with my big helpful heart.